I Got the Rhythm

Connie Schofield-Morrison · ILLUSTRATED BY Frank Morrison

SCHOLASTIC INC.

The beats to my drum, my hip-hops,
Nyree, Tyreek, Nia', Nasir, and Tiffani.
I LOVE U!
—C. S.-M.

I'm proud of you, Connie.
—F. M.

ISBN 978-0-545-83877-1

Text copyright © 2014 by Connie Schofield-Morrison.
Illustrations copyright © 2014 by Frank Morrison. All rights reserved.
Published by Scholastic Inc., 557 Broadway, New York, NY 10012,
by arrangement with Bloomsbury Children's Books. SCHOLASTIC and associated logos
are trademarks and/or registered trademarks of Scholastic Inc.

12 11 10 9 8 7 6 5 4 3 2   15 16 17 18 19 20/0

Printed in the U.S.A.   40

First Scholastic printing, January 2015

Art created with oil on canvas
Typeset in Elroy
Book design by Donna Mark and Yelena Safronova

I thought of a rhythm in my mind.

I heard the rhythm with my ears.

I looked at the rhythm with my eyes.

BLINK
BLINK

I smelled the rhythm with my nose.

I sang the rhythm with my mouth.

OOH LA LA

I caught the rhythm with my hands.

I kept the rhythm with my fingers.

I shook a rhythm with my hips.

I walked the rhythm with my feet.

I tapped the rhythm with my toes.

TIP TAP

I danced to the rhythm of a drum.

BEAT

I clapped and snapped,
I tipped and tapped.
I popped and locked,
I hipped and hopped.

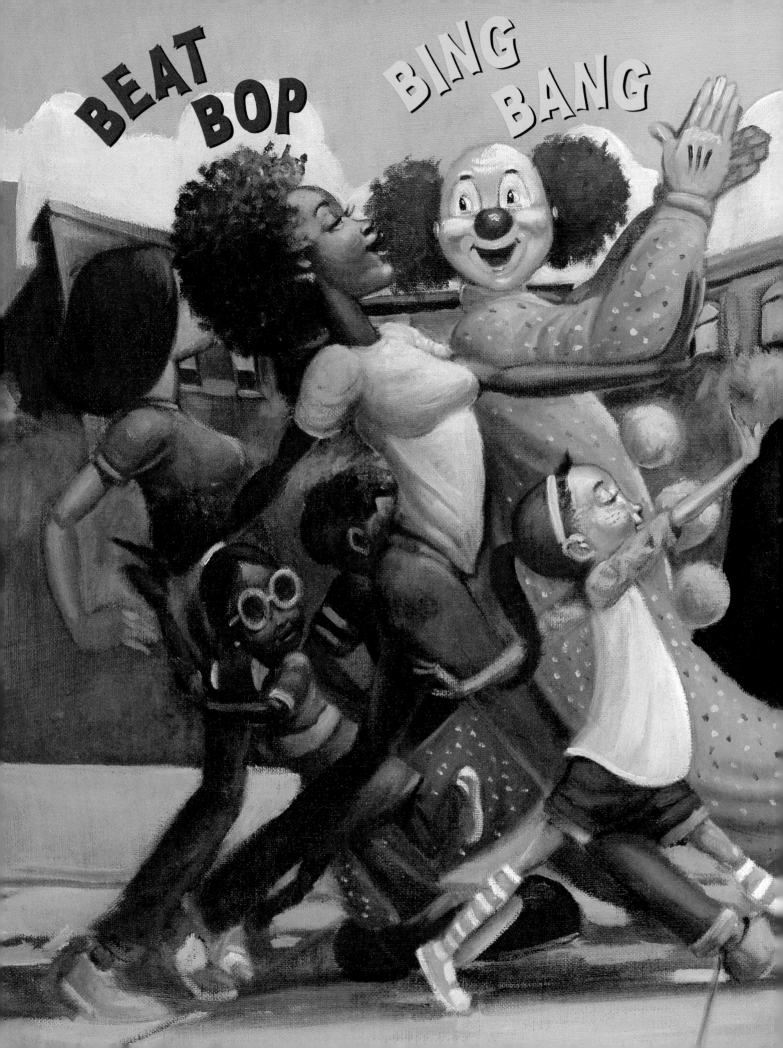

I got the rhythm and you can too.